HAUNTED HOUSES

BY
Lewann Sotnak

Illustrated by
Robert Andrew Parker

New York

Library of Congress Cataloging-in-Publication Data
Sotnak, Lewann.
　Haunted houses

　p. cm. — (Incredible histories)
　Includes bibliographical references.
　SUMMARY: Discusses the hauntings of various houses in England and the Soviet Union and throughout the United States, including the White House.
　ISBN 0-89686-508-8
　1. Haunted houses—Juvenile literature. 2. Ghosts—Juvenile literature. 3. Poltergeists—Juvenile literature. [1. Ghosts. 2. Poltergeists. 3. Supernatural.] I. Title. II. Series.
BF1475.S65 1990
133.1'22—dc20

　　　　　　　　　　　　　　　　　　　　　　　　　　　　　　　　　　　　89-70792
　　　　　　　　　　　　　　　　　　　　　　　　　　　　　　　　　　　　　　　CIP
　　　　　　　　　　　　　　　　　　　　　　　　　　　　　　　　　　　　　　　 AC

Illustration Credits
Cover: Kristi Schaeppi
Interior: Robert Andrew Parker

Copyright © 1990 by CRESTWOOD HOUSE, Macmillan Publishing Company

All rights reserved. No part of this book may be reproduced or transmitted in any form or by any means, electronic or mechanical, including photocopying, recording, or by any information storage and retrieval system, without permission in writing from the Publisher.

Macmillan Publishing Company
866 Third Avenue
New York, NY 10022
Collier Macmillan Canada, Inc.

Printed in the United States of America

First Edition

10 9 8 7 6 5 4 3 2 1

Contents

Spooky Dwellings 5

Borley Rectory 7

Ghosts in the White House 14

The Mysterious Bedroom 19

Popping Bottles 23

The Strange Presence in the Southwest Bedroom 27

The Dancing Poltergeist 31

Explainable Ghosts 35

Attempts to Understand Ghosts 38

For Further Reading 46

Index 47

Spooky Dwellings

Haunted house! The words bring shivers and a feeling of excitement. Stories about haunted houses have been around since people first began telling stories. They come from every corner of the world. Hauntings take place in big old houses, bright new apartment buildings, theaters, stores, Native American lodges, and log huts. There are stories of haunted swamps, woods, and roadsides. Ghosts have been reported in libraries, music buildings, and museums.

Ghosts and apparitions are usually quiet. They appear and disappear and move about soundlessly. Some hauntings are carried on by poltergeists. This is a German word that means noisy ghosts. Many people believe poltergeists are responsible for moving furniture and other objects and for noises that cannot be otherwise explained.

What makes people think a house is haunted? Sometimes it's the appearance of the house. It might be old and creepy. It might have a turret at the top. Or there might be a thick hedge growing around the house, with heavy vines trailing over the windows and porches. Although any place can be haunted, old houses are more apt to be. That's because more people have lived in them so there is a better chance that someone's ghost is still hanging around.

Reports of white, filmy ghosts or dark shadows moving through the rooms also make people think a house is haunted. People may have seen strange lights moving through halls or doorways. Or they say they have seen apparitions that look like people who have died. Frequently the ghosts are dressed in the clothes the deceased once wore.

Haunted places are also the sites of events that cannot be explained logically. Windows and doors open on their own; floorboards creak when no one appears to be there. Empty rocking chairs sway back and forth. Unexpected cold breezes and chilly spots touch the intruder. Moaning, stomping, whimpering, crying, walking, shuffling, rapping, and banging break the silence. Doorknobs rattle, bottles pop open, and plates fly across the room. Lights flick on and off when no one has touched a switch. Houses can be haunted in many different ways.

Everyone has to decide for herself or himself whether or not to believe in ghosts and haunted houses. But whatever they think, most people enjoy stories about spooky dwellings.

Borley Rectory

About 60 miles from London, there once stood what people called the most haunted house in England. Borley Rectory was a red brick building built in 1865 by the Reverend Henry Ellis Dawson Bull. It was to be a home for the church minister and his family.

From the beginning, strange things were seen at the rectory and nearby. In the garden around Borley, a mysterious, sad-faced nun was often seen strolling across the lawn. If anyone tried to get close enough to speak to her, she vanished. Just about everyone in the family saw her at some time or other, but no one was afraid of her.

After H. E. D. Bull died, his son, Harry Bull, became the rector. He also reported seeing ghosts around Borley. Since he joked a lot, no one knew whether to believe him. One day, however, three of Harry's sisters returned to Borley after a garden party. They saw the nun walking across the lawn. She carried her prayer beads in her hands.

One sister ran to find Elsie, the fourth sister. When Elsie tried to talk to the ghost, the nun disappeared. All the women noted that the nun looked very sad. Later, an investigator talked with three of the sisters separately. Their descriptions all matched.

Jokingly, Harry Bull once promised that after he died he would come back as a ghost if he did not like the minister who succeeded him. He promised he would haunt the rectory by throwing mothballs.

After Harry died, Borley stood vacant for a while. Then sure enough, people reported seeing mothballs flying through the empty rooms. Some claimed they saw Harry's ghost, too, dressed in a gray dinner jacket.

Fred Cartwright, a carpenter hired to repair some old farm buildings near the rectory, also sighted the spirit. He said that on his way to work, he saw the nun on the lawn of Borley.

People have wondered why the ghost was a nun. Some historians claim that in the 1200s, a convent or a monastery once stood where Borley was located. According to one story, a nun from a nearby convent tried to elope with the driver of a coach. When she was found, she was walled up alive in the convent.

In another version of the story, the nun tried to elope with a monk. When they were caught, the monk was hanged and the nun was walled up alive.

Some say the area around Borley was haunted, too. A man named Edward Cooper who worked for the rectory said that he and his wife began hearing strange sounds as soon as they moved into a small cottage near

the building in April 1916. Pattering feet, like those of a dog, kept them awake. But the strangest thing occurred one clear, moonlit night as the Coopers were getting ready for bed. Edward looked out the window. In the distance, he saw lights that appeared to be coming closer. Edward stood speechless as a black coach, drawn by two horses, pulled into view. On the seat were two figures in black top hats. Without a sound, the coach rushed by Edward's window. Then it glided through the hedge into the rectory yard where it disappeared. Other people also reported seeing the coach. Some said they heard hoofbeats but saw nothing. Others saw the coach but did not hear a sound.

Eric Smith and his family moved into Borley after it had stood empty awhile. They reported seeing apparitions and hearing footsteps and doorbells in the night. Alarmed, the Smiths called the newspaper and a ghost hunter named Harry Price. Mr. Price studied the situation but could not rid Borley of its hauntings. The Smiths decided they had had enough, so they moved out.

In October 1930, a new family came to Borley, Reverend Lionel Foyster and his young wife, Marianne. Poltergeists became extremely active after the Foysters moved in. Both the minister and his wife heard voices calling, "Marianne!" Marianne claimed that an invisible hand hit her and threw her out of bed. She said the mattress had tried to smother her. Then messages were scrawled on the wall and on pieces of paper. The messages asked for help, prayers, and light.

Once again Harry Price, the ghost hunter, was asked to come to the rectory. Harry believed in the existence of ghosts. But in this case, he did notice that much of the haunting activity took place, when Marianne was either out of sight or when she was all alone. That led some people to think that Marianne may have been bored and made up stories to get attention. Others thought that Marianne was emotionally troubled and imagined the hauntings. Still others said that she hated Borley and made up stories so her husband would agree to move out. Eventually the Foysters did move away, and Borley was empty once again.

Since no one wanted to buy the place, Harry Price then had his chance to investigate the rectory. He rented the house for one year. He brought in a team of psychic investigators, researchers, and interested students. During that year, strange things continued to happen. The nun was seen walking across the lawn. Two cold spots were discovered in the house. These areas stayed at 48 degrees Fahrenheit, no matter how warm it was elsewhere. Messages for Marianne kept appearing on the walls. Each message was circled and dated. A philosopher and psychologist from the University of London named Professor C. E. M. Joad

made the reports more believable when he testified that he had seen one of these messages. Harry Price then tried to convince more people by writing a book about all the strange happenings at Borley.

In 1939, a fire at Borley Rectory left standing only a burned-out shell. One report says the fire started when an oil lamp tipped over all by itself. People who watched the home burn said they saw strange figures rise out of the smoke. The ghost of a nun stood at an upstairs window.

After the fire, investigations continued. Harry Price had the ruins dug up. A human skull and some bones were discovered under the cellar floor. One scientist identified the skull as that of a young woman. Did it belong to the nun? Was she the ghost asking for help?

After Harry Price died, an English newspaper, the *Daily Mail,* claimed that Harry had made up the stories, and Mrs. Eric Smith, who had once lived at Borley, wrote and said that she didn't believe Borley was haunted. Most of the trouble came from bats, scratching rats, and curious sightseers, she claimed. Gradually Harry Price's reputation was tarnished and his book discredited.

Still people continue to visit the site. Some insist that they neither see ghosts nor feel their presence. Others claim there are strange temperature variations at Borley. They also say they hear unexplained noises and smell strange odors. Lights appear from no known source. Apparitions haunt the ruins. And so the arguments go on between those who believe Borley was and still is a haunted site and those who claim all such stories are a hoax.

Ghosts in the White House

What would you think if you saw Abraham Lincoln? Not just in a photograph or a movie, but the real man (or ghost) himself? Some people claim they have seen the ghost of President Lincoln. He has supposedly appeared to people both living at and visiting the White House.

People also claim that his death was foretold. In 1865, Lincoln made plans to attend a play Ford's Theater. A few days before, one of his bodyguards dreamed that Lincoln would be killed. He was so upset by the dream that he begged Lincoln not to attend the performance.

Lincoln also dreamed that an assassin would kill him. In the dream, he saw himself lying in a coffin. But historians point out that Lincoln was a gloomy man. He often brooded over the possibility of being assassinated. In the early morning of the day of the performance, Lincoln dreamed that he was on a ship sailing to an unknown place. That night he was shot and killed while he watched a play.

After his death, people began hearing his footsteps walking through the halls of the White House.

President Calvin Coolidge's wife, Grace Coolidge, is one of the people who said she saw Lincoln's ghost. One day when she was walking up to the White House, she glanced up at the Oval Office. Her heart jumped. There she saw Lincoln standing in the window. He stared right at her, then turned and walked away.

There were frequent reports of Lincoln's ghost during the presidency of Franklin Delano Roosevelt. Roosevelt's secretaries supposedly either saw the ghost or felt its presence.

One time Queen Wilhelmina of the Netherlands visited the White House. She was comfortably settled in her bedroom when suddenly there was a knock on her door. "Come in," she called. No one responded, so the queen got up and opened the door. There stood Abraham Lincoln in his top hat. One report says Queen Wilhelmina was so frightened that she fainted. When she came to, the figure was gone.

The queen told President Roosevelt about her experience the next morning. He told her that several people had reported seeing Lincoln in that same bedroom. In fact, it is known as the Lincoln Room.

Several workers at the White House reported seeing Lincoln sitting on the bed in the Lincoln Room, pulling on his boots. One of these was Mrs. Eleanor Roosevelt's maid, Mary Eban. One night when Mrs. Roosevelt was working late, Mary Eban came rushing in to her. The maid said she had seen Lincoln sitting on the bed taking off his boots.

Many people who cannot claim to have seen the ghost of Lincoln say they have felt his presence. And Roosevelt's little dog, Fala, often barked at something no one else could see. Could it have been Abe's ghost?

President Harry Truman used to say that he heard many mysterious knocks on his door in the middle of the night. When he answered, no one was ever there. Truman joked about these incidents. He said it must have been Lincoln knocking. Truman didn't believe in ghosts, but he heard the knocks.

Some people say that after President Truman's term ended, Lincoln's ghost seemed to disappear from the

White House for a time. However, there are recent stories from the administration of former President Ronald Reagan. His daughter, Maureen, and her husband, Dennis Revell, usually slept in the Lincoln Room when they visited the White House. Maureen insisted that sometimes in the early morning hours she and Dennis saw a red or orange aura. They strongly felt that it was Lincoln's spirit. Ronald and Nancy Reagan weren't so sure they believed in the ghost. Nancy said she never heard Lincoln knocking on her door. But she did admit that the family dog, Rex, often barked at the door of the Lincoln Room.

Lincoln's ghost has not been the only apparition floating about the White House. At one time, Dolly Madison's ghost caused quite a stir in the gardens. Dolly Madison was the wife of James Madison, fourth president of the United States.

When the Madisons lived in the White House, Dolly had planted a beautiful rose garden. She loved the garden and often walked through it to admire the roses. About 100 years after Dolly's death, her ghost appeared to the gardeners who worked for President Woodrow Wilson. Apparently Mrs. Wilson didn't want to keep the rose garden and had ordered it to be dug up. That's when Mrs. Madison's ghost began to bother the gardeners. They were sure she was warning them not to disturb her roses. So the garden stayed.

The ghosts of other presidents have also been seen or heard. One night a seamstress was working late in the Rose Room, which had once been President Andrew Jackson's bedroom. Suddenly the seamstress heard laughter. No one was nearby. Then a strange chill surrounded her for just a moment. Had Jackson's ghost paid a visit?

William Henry Harrison, ninth president of the United States, died after only one month in office. There were many stories about his ghostly visits to the attic before the White House was remodeled.

One wonders if the White House ghosts ever bump into each other in the halls or fight over who gets to haunt which room.

The Mysterious Bedroom

One hot August night in 1960, in Prescott, Wisconsin, George Wolf lay on his bed, trying to sleep. He listened to the crickets and tree frogs making their summer music. Suddenly he heard the sound of slippered

feet pacing in Uncle Otto's room, which was next to his own. The floorboards creaked as the feet went back and forth. The only problem was that Uncle Otto had been dead for two years.

George crept down the hall and opened the door to the room. He saw nothing. Everything was exactly as it had been when Uncle Otto died in 1958. Otto had lived with the Wolfs for 26 years. He was a kind man who had been an important part of the family. In the last years of his life, because of blindness and frail health, he had spent a good deal of time in his bedroom. He often paced the floor at night when he couldn't sleep.

Now, two years later, the pacing started again. Every time George went to investigate, the noise stopped. George wondered if the noise was caused by mice, squirrels, or the Siamese cats in the house. One night he sprinkled flour around the room and checked for paw prints the next morning. There were none.

Another night when George passed Uncle Otto's room, the door was slightly open. George glanced in. The rocking chair was moving back and forth, very slowly. The rocker had been Uncle Otto's favorite chair. George checked to see if a breeze or the cats were moving it. He could find nothing.

Still another evening, someone accidentally shut one of the cats in Uncle Otto's room. The next morning, George's mother found a terrified cat sitting in the middle of the room. Its eyes were wide, and the fur stood straight up from its back. The cat never went upstairs again.

No one in the family felt afraid, however. The uncle had always been such a kindly man that they were sure his ghost would never cause any harm.

Some authorities on the subject say that ghost activity increases when hard times such as illness or financial disaster come to a family. That may have been true for the Wolfs. Not long after the haunting began, George's parents, Carl and Marian Wolf, began having health problems that cost them a lot of money. By December 1967, the family decided to sell the house so they could pay the bills. Apparently Uncle Otto's ghost was not happy with this decision. One morning George and his parents awoke to a pounding from Uncle Otto's room, which sounded like a giant handball bouncing off the walls. Shortly after the house was sold, the poundings and knockings grew worse and spread from his room to other rooms.

Then a few weeks before the family moved, an unbelievable incident occurred. George was reading in his room when suddenly he heard a tremendous splintering sound. He ran out into the hallway and looked toward Uncle Otto's room. The huge oak door of the room was being pulled slowly from its hinges. It was as if invisible hands were ripping at the door frame. Mrs.

Wolf rushed upstairs, too, just in time to see the huge oak door thrown into the middle of the hallway. Heavy bolts hung from the broken door frame.

During its eight years of haunting, Uncle Otto's ghost never touched any of the family. But on one of the last mornings he lived in the house, George was awakened by a soft brushing against his face. It felt like a human hand touching his cheek. At first, George thought it was one of the cats. He turned on the light. There sat the cat in an old chair, its back arched. Its frightened eyes followed the movement across the room of something George could not see. Then it was gone. George believed that Uncle Otto had come to say good-bye. That was the last the family felt or heard from his ghost.

Popping Bottles

On February 3, 1958, strange things began happening in the Long Island, New York, home of Mr. and Mrs. James Herrmann and their children, James, 12, and Lucille, 13. Bottles around the house started popping their tops and pouring out their contents. Each day new bottles popped open and spilled: holy water in the master bedroom, bottles of shampoo in the bathroom, stomach medicine in the medicine cabinet, liquid starch under the sink, and bleach in the basement.

At first Mr. and Mrs. Herrmann thought the children were pulling pranks. But James and Lucille declared they were innocent. Besides, when all the activity started, James came home from school and found a ceramic doll and ship model broken on the dresser in his room. He wouldn't wreck his own property.

One Sunday the family was eating together in the dining room. Noises began coming from some of the other rooms. The Herrmanns investigated and found that once again the holy water had spilled. Liquid starch was running all over the kitchen floor. James and Lucille had been with their parents, so this time they could not be blamed.

Later in the day, Mr. Herrmann happened to pass the bathroom, where James was brushing his teeth. Mr. Herrmann paused for a few seconds. Then his hair nearly stood on end. He saw two bottles, one of shampoo and the other of medicine, slide in opposite directions and fall off the table. Mr. Herrmann called the police. Officers came out and interviewed the family. They searched the house. A detective was assigned to the house full-time. The bottles kept popping their tops and spilling their contents. As if that weren't enough,

the furniture and other objects began to move about. The police studied, tested, and searched. They set up an oscillograph, which measured the tiniest vibrations in the basement. Spilled liquids were analyzed for unusual contents in the police laboratory. The power company checked the ground wiring and fuses. Every household appliance was thoroughly examined. No one found anything out of the ordinary in any of these investigations.

Next a cap was put on the chimney to keep the wind from coming in and blowing objects around. Scientists, engineers, and other specialists came to explore the strange activities. They tested the house for settling. Maps were examined for underground streams. The area was checked for radio frequencies. Plumbers looked to see if there were unexpected vibrations. Even flight schedules of the nearby airfield were investigated to see if there was any correlation between airplane takeoffs and the weird happenings in the house. No connection was found. The experts were baffled.

Meanwhile the activity increased. More bottles popped and spilled. Porcelain figurines flew off their tables and broke. Furniture moved and fell over. By now the Parapsychology Laboratory of Duke University became involved. They made charts and diagrams. They drew arrows to show where and what distances the objects moved. They added chemicals to the household bottles but could not cause them to unfasten their tops.

Then on March 10, objects stopped flying as quickly as they had started. The scientists left with no answers. The mystery was never solved.

The Strange Presence in the Southwest Bedroom

Can a house be haunted even before it is built? In 1893, Jimmy Jensen began to build a farmhouse for his family on a hilltop near Albert Lea, a small town in southern Minnesota. A log cabin had once stood on the site. But the entire time Jimmy worked on the house he felt uneasy. Something was wrong in the area of the southwest bedroom. There seemed to be a presence there that looked over his shoulder the whole time he worked.

Jimmy Jensen finished the house, and he and his family lived in it for 53 years. But during that whole time, no one ever used the southwest bedroom. The presence continued to frighten everyone who tried to sleep there.

In 1946, the family finally moved out. For the next 17 years, 14 different people moved in and out of the house. No one stayed long, and the neighbors were puzzled.

Finally in 1963, Dick and Anita Borland bought the house. By then its windows were broken, the paint was peeling, and the porches sagged. But the Borlands had nine children and were excited about all the space. They happily remodeled the place.

Just before the Borlands moved in, however, one of Anita Borland's sisters-in-law saw someone on the upstairs porch outside the southwest bedroom. She thought the woman looked like Anita's mother. Anita agreed, but when she and her two sisters-in-law went upstairs to greet the visitor, no one was there.

About half a year later, the Borland children began meeting the presence. One day two of them met a woman upstairs in the hallway. She was tall and thin and wore a flowered print dress with an apron. Since the hallway was rather dark, the children thought at first that the woman was their mother. But then the stranger cried out for help.

The children raced down to the kitchen where they found their mother. They told her about the strange lady in the upstairs hall. But when Anita and her children went back upstairs, the stranger had vanished.

Several weeks later, two of the Borland girls, sleeping in the southwest bedroom, awoke to see the ghost of the same woman in the flowered dress. The figure was standing in the closet. A light glowed above her head, even though the closet had no lights! The woman came out of the closet, shook the bed, and disappeared.

Sometimes when she was alone, Theresa, who liked to read in the southwest bedroom, said she felt a cold hand on her bare foot. Cold fingers closed over her instep and jerked her foot back and forth. One night her 17-year-old brother, Christopher, felt someone bounce on his bed. At first he thought it was his sister Nancy, trying to annoy him. He stretched out his body and pushed at her with his foot. But something pushed back. It wasn't Nancy. It wasn't anyone! Christopher jumped from the bed and ran screaming from the room.

The ghost in the flowered dress wasn't the only presence in that household. One day Anita met an old woman in her kitchen. Anita was about to offer her a cup of coffee when she faded away.

Anita asked one of Jimmy Jensen's daughters, who

was born in the house in 1906, about the old woman. She convinced Anita that the ghost was that of Grandma Jensen, who had died in the house. Grandma Jensen had spent a good deal of time in the pantry area.

The ghost of the pantry appeared several times and then stopped coming around. But the ghost in the flowered dress still lingers. Could it be a woman who lived in the log cabin that once stood on that site?

The Dancing Poltergeist

One of the eeriest haunted house tales comes from the Soviet Union, or Russia, as it was called in 1870. The strange events began happening at a country estate in the Uralsk province near Orensburg. Maria, the cook, had just put the small daughter of Helena and Gregor Schapoff to bed. The child had been fussy, so Maria had played the harmonica and entertained her with a brisk three-step dance. That always put the little girl to sleep.

On her own way to bed, Maria stopped to say good night to Helena, who was talking with a friend in the living room. After Maria left, Helena and her friend continued to chat. Suddenly they heard rapping in the walls. Then the rhythm changed to a lively three-step dance. At first they thought it was Maria. Then they realized the noise was coming from the attic—where Maria could not have gone without again passing through the living room.

Helena and her guest checked Maria's room. She was sound asleep. The frightened women started for the attic, lanterns in hand. They searched the dusty corners but found no source of the dancing. Now the rapping and dancing sounds went ahead of them. They shook the walls and rattled the windows. Soon the whole household awoke, but no one found anything or anyone to account for the sounds.

Gregor Schapoff heard about the strange happening when he returned from a business trip. The miller suggested that the noise might have come from a pigeon. He had knocked down a nest from under the eaves earlier and thought the bird might have gotten into the house. Gregor happily accepted this sensible explanation.

After dismissing the household, he settled comfortably in his chair. Around 10 P.M. he heard scratching noises, then the sound of a perfect three-step dance.

"Helena must be trying to tease me," he muttered. He went up to the bedroom to scold her, but he found his wife asleep.

Gregor heard more dancing steps and then loud raps that awakened Helena. He grabbed his gun from the drawer, roused his servants, and set out to find the intruder. But they found nothing.

The next night, Gregor invited some neighbors to come hear the dancing. It went on all night and nearly knocked a door off its hinges before it stopped. The next week, some nights were quiet, but others echoed with dancing sounds. Guests came to witness the strange event. Stories of the dancing ghost spread. Scientists and spiritualists came to study the situation, and the event was reported to the governor of the province. He appointed a committee to investigate. The committee believed that Helena was tricking everyone into believing the noise was a ghost. The governor sent a sharp warning to stop the nonsense.

As if in response, the poltergeist started fires in Helena's closet and under her mattress. One day her dress burst into flames. Onlookers beat out the flames and badly burned their hands, but somehow the fire did not touch Helena. She didn't have so much as a blister.

Finally Gregor and Helena had had enough. They moved back to their other home in Iletski. And that was the end of the dancing poltergeist.

Explainable Ghosts

Suppose you are all alone in a house. It is night, and the weather is stormy. You hear scratching, scraping, and rattling. You see shadows moving. Even if you think you don't believe in ghosts, questions gnaw at you. Maybe, just maybe, there are ghosts after all.

People often give ghosts the credit for haunting a place when something from the natural world causes the activity. The wind sighs mournfully through cracks or down the chimney. Pebbles fall off the roof. Spirals of rising fog create ghostly shapes.

There are also people who like to fool others. They do tricks with their cameras, such as creating double exposures. Neither one is clear, which may give the illusion of a strange presence in the picture or objects floating in space.

Some "ghosts" are simply imagined. People who are deeply troubled may imagine things that aren't there at all. Those who use alcohol or drugs to alter their minds may also think they see things that don't exist.

It also happens that some people see things others don't. Think of what happens when people report an

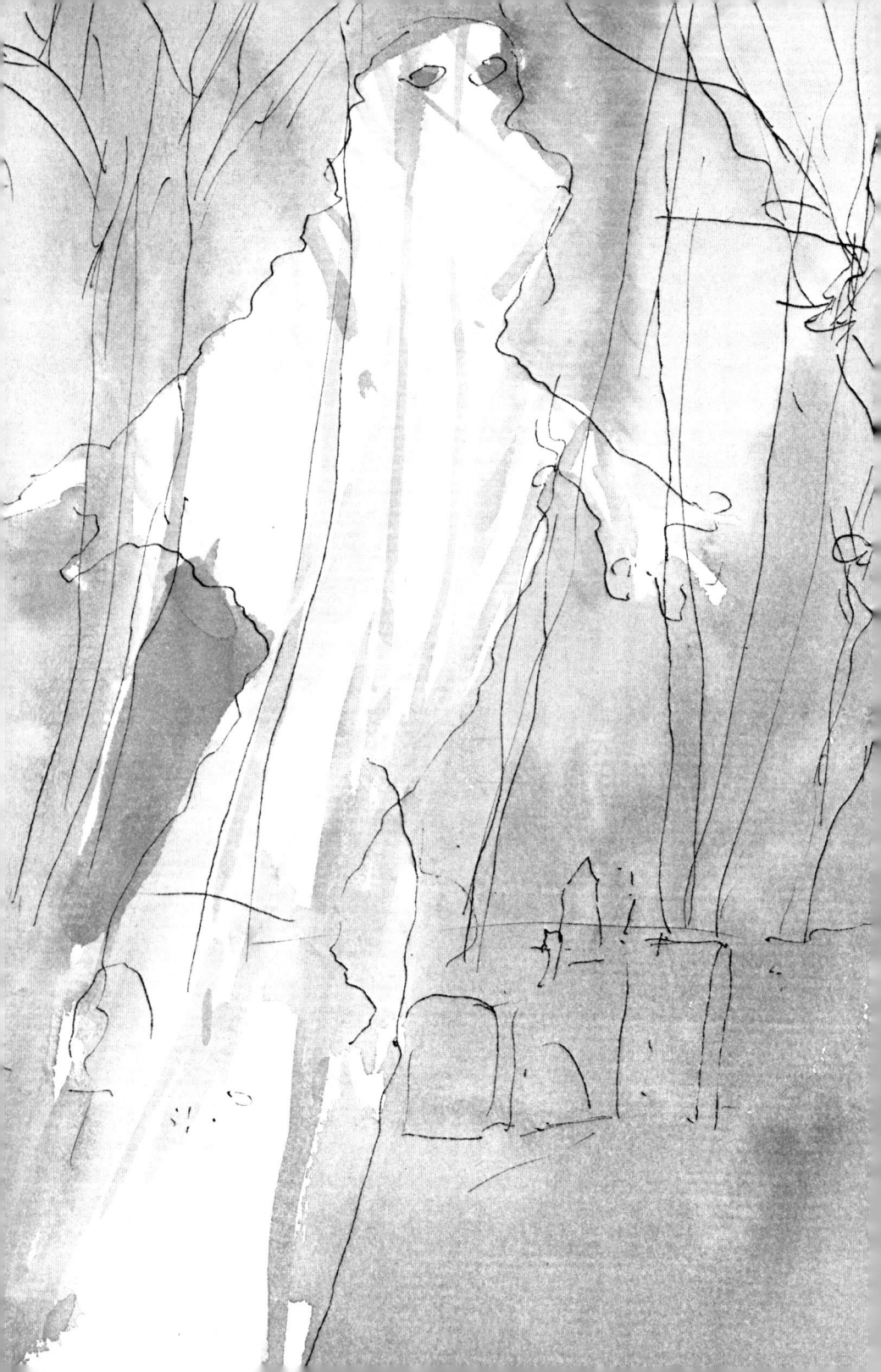

accident or similar event. Five people may give five different stories of what they think really happened. So when something strange occurs, individuals see and hear it differently. Those with vivid imaginations see more in an event than others. If one really wishes to see a ghost, chances are that he or she will see one.

Attempts to Understand Ghosts

What things are real? Are they only what we can experience with our five senses or measure in a laboratory? Some people are said to have a sixth sense. This means they have the ability to sense what the average person cannot. Many people believe that there are dimensions of reality that stretch beyond our physical world.

Parapsychology is the study of behavior that goes beyond what we think is normal or possible. This behavior is also called paranormal. Psychics are people who are especially sensitive to paranormal phenomena. There are organizations all over the world devoted to the study of parapsychology. One of the best known places for this in the United States is Duke University. J. B. Rhine and his wife, Louisa E. Rhine, became famous for their studies in parapsychology, which they began at Duke in the 1930s.

William Roll and J. Gaither Pratt, investigators from the Parapsychology Laboratory of Duke University, were called in to try to solve the bottle-popping mystery at the Herrmann household in 1958. They worked on

other strange cases as well. One of the devices they used for testing was called a PK machine. PK stands for psychokinesis, which means "moved by the mind." Psycho means "of the mind." Kinesis means "motion." A fascinating question parapsychologists are trying to answer is whether or not one can move objects by using the mind alone. PK machines shake and roll dice. The person being tested tries to concentrate on how he or she wants the dice to fall. The idea is to see if it is possible to influence the way they land. Until now there has been no agreement on whether they actually affect the results.

A psychic investigator, Gertrude Schmeidler, tested for a ghost in a haunted house. She had an architect make a careful floor plan of the place. The family who lived in the house checked off the places where they had seen or felt the ghost. Then Schmeidler gave unmarked floor plans to nine psychics. They toured the house and marked the locations that they felt were haunted. The results showed that a significant number of psychics sensed the ghost in the same places that the family did.

Michaeleen Maher, another psychic, expanded on Schmeidler's experiment by doing a similar test in a haunted apartment. This time she handed both psychics and skeptics (nonbelievers) an unmarked floor plan and had them mark the haunted spots. The results of her experiment were similar to Schmeidler's.

Maher also developed a machine that generates random numbers. If something abnormal is present, that presence may interfere with the number patterns and cause a red light to flash. The test did show that the light flashed more often than would be ordinarily expected, suggesting that there might be some kind of presence. Maher claims that many more tests are needed to prove anything.

Some researchers have tried using Geiger counters to test for ghosts. When these devices encounter radioactive presence, they beep or click more rapidly. The problem with using them to detect ghosts is that there may be other things around the house that are radioactive.

T. C. Lethbridge, an archaeologist, explorer, and psychic, had a theory that ghosts might be pictures projected by someone else's mind. The person seeing the ghost, then, was the receiving set. He or she needed to be on the right wavelength for the experience to happen. This suggests that ghosts and apparitions are the result of mental telepathy (sending messages directly from one mind to another without any other communication).

Another theory that has been proposed by psychics is that people make impressions on their homes, furniture, clothes, and other objects that they own. When they die these impressions or memories are still stored in the old possessions. These things can play back the memories like movies, tapes, or discs, making the ghosts appear.

Modern technology has also been making its way into the study of haunted houses. Professor Charles Tart of the University of California says that electronic sensing devices and computers might show whether or not the ghost phenomenon is real. The future may hold a number of possibilities. Various detectors with filters might be able to monitor different parts of the electromagnetic field where ghost activity could be taking place. Transducers could detect even the tiniest bit of light or other energy given off by a ghost. Electronic devices and filters might detect sounds that cannot be heard by the human ear. Heat sensors or infrared equipment could record exact temperature changes in the haunted area. The right kind of gauges may be able to detect movement and the force that caused that movement. Various sensors could be attached to observers to measure body responses when a person claims to see a ghost. Other things that might be measured are radio waves, odors, chemical content of the air, magnetic files, and radiation levels. Professor Tart suggests that by connecting all these sensors to a computer that can record changes moment by moment, we might be able to see patterns that will give us clues about ghosts.

Ray Hyman, professor of psychology at the University of Oregon, points out the difficulty in investigating something such as a ghost in a haunted house. He says that when someone sees a ghost, the investigation takes place afterward. There is no way to anticipate the event in order to devise a way of proving that it actually happened. Nor is there a way to set up controls to repeat or measure the event. The investigator must rely on what the person has said. Hyman also points out that the field of parapsychology has no textbooks in which repeated experiments can be collected and analyzed.

Many religions teach that a person's consciousness (or soul) is separate from his or her body. After one dies, that consciousness still exists. Some psychics believe a ghost or an apparition is a consciousness that is still strongly connected to the events, people, or possessions in this life. After death it is not ready to let go of these things. When this is the case, some psychics claim that the soul might overlap with our space. They suggest that when a person dies before his or her time, or by violence, such a death can produce energy that leaves psychic imprints that last for a long time.

Poltergeist activity possibly comes from people who build up a tremendous amount of psychic energy. Investigators who have tested such people often find that they have a lot of anger and resentment built up inside, which they are unable to express. Or perhaps they are experiencing severe mental stress. Usually the activity centers around a young person, often in the midteens. This is a time of strong emotional energy and change that may cause strange physical events in the form of released energy. It might even make objects and furniture move on their own.

When ghosts haunt a house, psychics or mediums (ghost busters) are sometimes called. These people walk about the area and try to sense where the ghosts are. They try to talk to a ghost and ask why it is there. Sometimes the ghost buster burns sage to help communicate with the presence. At other times the ghost or apparition is ordered to leave. And sometimes it does!

For Further Reading

Cohen, Daniel. *America's Very Own Ghosts.* New York: Dodd, Mead & Company, 1985.

———. *The World's Most Famous Ghosts.* New York: Dodd, Mead & Company, 1978.

Deem, James. *How to Find a Ghost.* Boston: Houghton Mifflin Company, 1988.

Edmonds, I. G. *The Girls Who Talked to Ghosts: The Story of Katie and Margaretta Fox.* New York: Rinehart & Winston, 1979.

Kettlekamp, Larry. *Haunted Houses.* New York: William Morrow and Company, 1969.

Roop, Peter and Connie. *Poltergeists, Great Mysteries, Opposing Viewpoints.* St. Paul, Minnesota: Greenhaven Press, Inc., 1988.

Taves, Isabella. *True Ghost Stories.* New York: Franklin Watts, 1978.

Williams, Gurney, III. *Ghosts and Poltergeists.* New York: Franklin Watts, 1979.

Index

Albert Lea, Minnesota 27
apparitions 5, 6, 10, 14, 18, 41, 44, 45

Borland family 29–31
Borley Rectory 7, 8, 10–11, 13–14
Bull family 7–8

Cartwright, Fred 8
cold spots 11
Coolidge, President and Mrs. Calvin 15
Cooper, Edward 8, 10

Duke University 38

Eban, Mary 16
electromagnetic 42
electronic technology 42
exorcism

Foyster, Rev. Kionel and Marianne 10, 11

Geiger counters 41
ghostbusters 45

heat sensors 42
Herrmann family 23–24, 38
Hyman, Ray 44

infrared equipment 42
Iletski 34

Jackson, President Andrew 19
Jensen, Jimmy 27, 29, 30
Joad, Professor C. E. M. 11

Lethbridge, T. C. 41
Lincoln, Abraham 14–16
London, England 7
Long Island, New York 23

Madison, President James and Mrs. Dolly 18
Maher, Michaeleen 40–41

47

mental telepathy 41

Netherlands 15

Orensburg 31
oscillograph 26

parapsychology 38, 40, 44
Parapsychology Laboratory of Duke University 26, 38
poltergeists 5, 10, 31, 34, 44
Pratt, J. Gaither 38
Prescott, Wisconsin 19
Price Harry 10, 11, 13
psychics 11, 38, 40, 41, 44, 45
psychokinesis (PK) machine 40

Reagan, President Ronald and Mrs. Nancy 18
Revell, Dennis and Maureen 18
Rhine, J.B. and Louisa E. 38

Roll, William 38
Roosevelt, President Franklin Delano and Mrs. Eleanor 15, 16

Schapoff, Gregor and Helena 31, 33–34
Schmeidler, Gertrude 40
Smith, Eric 10, 13

Tart, Professor Charles 42
transducers 42
Truman, President Harry 16

Uncle Otto 21–23
Uralsk, Soviet Union 31

White House 14, 15, 18, 19
Wilhelmina, Queen 15–16
Wilson, President Woodrow and Mrs. 18
Wolf, Carl and Marian 22–23
Wolf, George 19, 21–23